I Am Strong

A POSITIVE POWER STORY

by Suzy Capozzi

illustrated by Eren Unten

Random House 🏠 New York

Today is field day.
I wake up early
to get ready.

I lace up
my new sneakers.

Dad makes a big,
healthy breakfast.
I feel strong.

All the students
head to the big field.
Captains get picked.
Teams get picked next.

One by one,
everyone joins their team.

Joe picks me.
I am excited.
I know I can help
the blue team.

I am faster
than I look.
I am strong, too.

First up is
the relay race.
We have five minutes
to warm up.
I know what to do!

I show my team
how to pass the baton.

The race starts.
I cheer on my team.

Now it's my turn.
I hold tight, run fast, and pass it carefully.
We finish strong.

We go to our next event.
It is a huge puzzle.
The pieces are bulky.
Everyone is rushing to put
the puzzle together.

I try to help.
I step back and look.
I see the solution.

"It's just like passing the baton," I say.
"Slow down and work together."

We work together.
We finish the puzzle.
We are a strong team.

It is time for
the three-legged race.
Ana and I are partners.

Some people laugh.
They call us "short stuff."
But we are a good match.

Other teams stumble and fall.
Ana and I are in step.
We get faster as we go.

Our size is our strength
and we win!

We head to the next event.
It's the water balloon toss.
I know I can do this.

I know it!

I get three tries.
My first shot is too high.
My second one goes
off course.

I take my last shot.
I pull back as far as I can.
Bull's-eye!

It is time for
our last event—
the obstacle course.
Three teams are tied
for first place.

My team has a plan.
We will do each obstacle
together as a team.

FINISH

We help each other
climb the ropes up and
down the wall.

We wait and cheer
as everyone hops
through the hoops.

We go slow and steady
on the wavy beam.

We take the lead
on the ski boards.

The blue team crosses
the finish line together!

Today is a great day!
I helped the team in
every way I could.
I never gave up.
I am strong!

For Liz, the Strong
—S.C.
To Melissa, with love
—E.U.

All rights reserved. Published in the United States by Random House Children's Books, a division of Penguin Random House LLC, New York. Originally published by Rodale Kids, an imprint of Random House Children's Books, a division of Penguin Random House LLC, New York, in 2018.

Step into Reading, Random House, and the Random House colophon are registered trademarks of Penguin Random House LLC.

Visit us on the Web!
StepIntoReading.com
rhcbooks.com

Educators and librarians, for a variety of teaching tools, visit us at
RHTeachersLibrarians.com

Library of Congress Cataloging-in-Publication Data is available upon request.
ISBN 978-0-593-48180-6 (trade) — ISBN 978-0-593-48181-3 (lib. bdg.) —
ISBN 978-0-593-48182-0 (ebook)

Printed in the United States of America
10 9 8 7 6 5 4 3 2 1

This book has been officially leveled by using the F&P Text Level Gradient™ Leveling System.

FEB 1 0 2004

DATE DUE

MAR 0 5 2004		
JAN 2 6 2006		
JAN 2 8 2016		
MAR 2 5 2019		
APR 2 9 2019		

Demco, Inc. 38-293

PATTERNS
What's on the Wall?

Based on the Math Monsters™ public television series,
developed in cooperation with the National Council
of Teachers of Mathematics (NCTM).

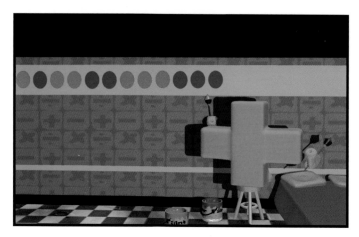

by John Burstein

Reading consultant: Susan Nations, M.Ed., author/literacy coach/consultant

Math curriculum consultants: Marti Wolfe, M.Ed., teacher/presenter; Kristi Hardi-Gilson, B.A., teacher/presenter

WEEKLY WR READER®
EARLY LEARNING LIBRARY

Please visit our web site at: **www.earlyliteracy.cc**
For a free color catalog describing Weekly Reader® Early Learning Library's list
of high-quality books, call 1-877-445-5824 (USA) or 1-800-387-3178 (Canada).
Weekly Reader® Early Learning Library's fax: (414) 336-0164.

Library of Congress Cataloging-in-Publication Data

Burstein, John.
　　Patterns: what's on the wall? / by John Burstein.
　　　　p. cm. — (Math monsters)
　　Summary: The four math monsters show how to make different kinds of patterns
as they paint their walls.
　　ISBN 0-8368-3816-5 (lib. bdg.)
　　ISBN 0-8368-3831-9 (softcover)
　　1. Pattern perception—Juvenile literature. [1. Pattern perception.] I. Title.
　BF294.B87　2003
　152.14'23—dc21
2003045039

This edition first published in 2004 by
Weekly Reader® Early Learning Library
330 West Olive Street, Suite 100
Milwaukee, WI　53212　USA

Text and artwork copyright © 2004 by Slim Goodbody Corp. (www.slimgoodbody.com).
This edition copyright © 2004 by Weekly Reader® Early Learning Library.

Original Math Monsters™ animation: Destiny Images
Art direction, cover design, and page layout: Tammy Gruenewald
Editor: JoAnn Early Macken

Printed in the United States of America

1 2 3 4 5 6 7 8 9 07 06 05 04 03

You can enrich children's mathematical experience by working with
them as they tackle the Corner Questions in this book. Create
a special notebook for recording their mathematical ideas.

Patterns and Math

Creating and describing patterns are important mathematical skills.
Because patterns are part of a child's everyday experience, they can
be a wonderful doorway into exploring mathematical ideas.

Meet the Math Monsters™

ADDISON

Addison thinks
math is fun.
"I solve problems
one by one."

Mina flies
from here to there.
"I look for answers
everywhere."

MINA

MULTIPLEX

Multiplex
sure loves to laugh.
"Both my heads
have fun with math."

Split is friendly
as can be.
"If you need help,
then count on me."

SPLIT

**We're glad you want to take a look
at the story in our book.**

**We know that as you read, you'll see
just how helpful math can be.**

**Let's get started. Jump right in!
Turn the page, and let's begin!**

Split was at home in the Math Monsters' castle. She looked around her room. She said, "I will make this room look pretty. I will paint a pattern on the wall."

As she painted, she sang,
"Triangle, circle, heart, square —
I will paint these shapes and then
— triangle, circle, heart, square —
I will paint them over again."
Split painted her pattern over
and over.

Multiplex came in.

*Have you ever
made a pattern
with shapes?*

5

"Telephone call for you, Split," said Multiplex.

"I am too busy painting patterns to talk right now," said Split.

"I can help you," said Multiplex. "I will paint, and you can talk."

"Thank you," said Split. "Will you keep my pattern going?"

"I will do my best," said Multiplex.

Split went to answer the phone.

What will Multiplex do?

7

"Split has made a pattern using shapes," said Multiplex. "To keep her pattern going, I will paint shapes, too."

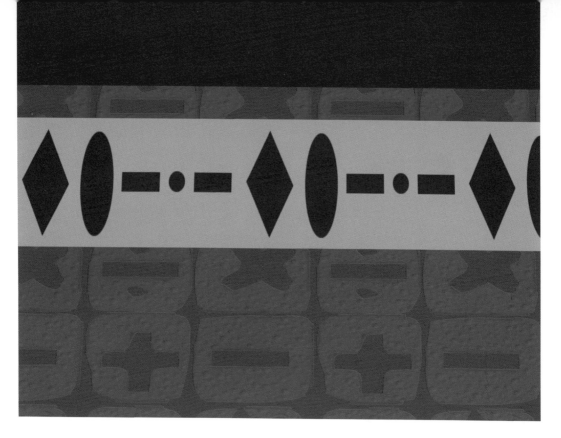

Multiplex picked up the brush.
As he painted, he sang,
   "Rhombus, oval, dash, dot, dash —
   I will paint these shapes, and then
   — rhombus, oval, dash, dot, dash —
   I will paint them over again."

Is Multiplex following Split's pattern?

Mina flew in. She looked at Split's pattern. She looked at the shapes Multiplex was painting.

"Multiplex, you are not keeping the pattern going," she said.

"I am painting shapes," said Multiplex.

"They are not the same shapes Split painted," said Mina. "To keep her pattern going, you must use only her shapes."

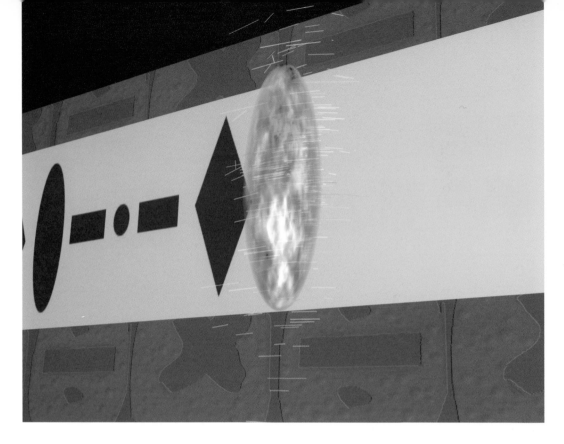

"Oh," said Multiplex. "I will use some monster magic to take away what I painted. Then you can show me what to do."

What do you think Mina will paint?

Mina began to paint and sing.
"Heart, circle, square, triangle —
I will paint these shapes, and then
— heart, circle, square, triangle —
I will paint them over again."
Mina painted her pattern over and over again.
Addison came in.

Addison looked at the pattern Mina was painting.

"Mina, you are not keeping Split's pattern going," he said.

"She used the same shapes as Split," said Multiplex. "What can be wrong?"

Mina and Split used the same shapes. How is Mina's pattern different?

"Look at the pattern Split painted," he said. "First there was a triangle, then a circle, then a heart, and then a square. You painted the same shapes, but you did not paint them in the same order."

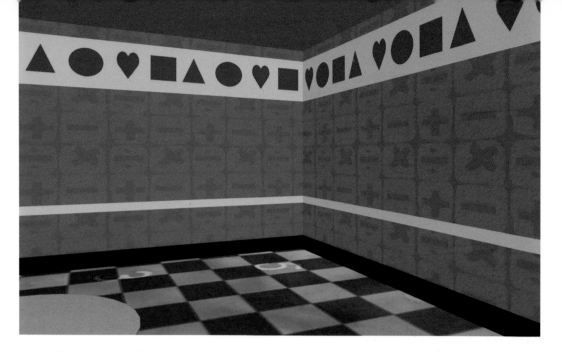

"Oh, I see," said Multiplex. "To keep a pattern going, you must use the same shapes and paint them in the same order."

"I will use monster magic and start over," said Mina. "I will paint the same shapes. This time, I will paint them in the right order. First a triangle, then a circle, then a heart, and then a square."

What kind of pattern can you make with four shapes? What about five?

Addison went to his own room. "I will paint a new pattern," he said.

He painted one red circle and one blue circle. Then he painted two red circles.

"That is pretty," said Split,
"but it is not a pattern."
"Yes it is," said Addison.
"Watch what I paint next."

What do you think Addison will paint next?

Addison painted two more blue circles.

Then he painted three more
red circles.
"Can you see my pattern?"
he asked.

What do you think Addison will paint next?

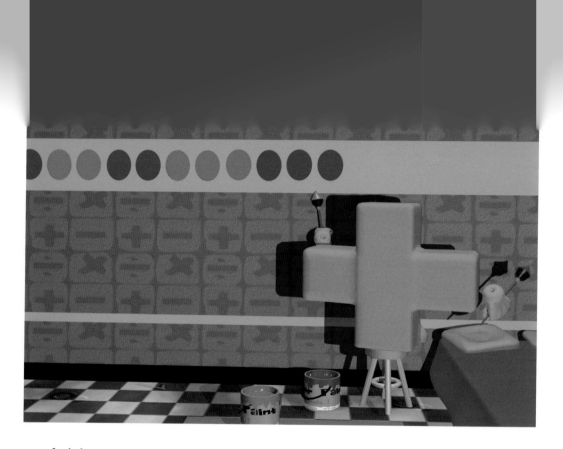

Addison painted three more blue circles.

"I see your pattern," said Split. "You keep adding circles."

"Yes," said Addison. "My pattern is growing."

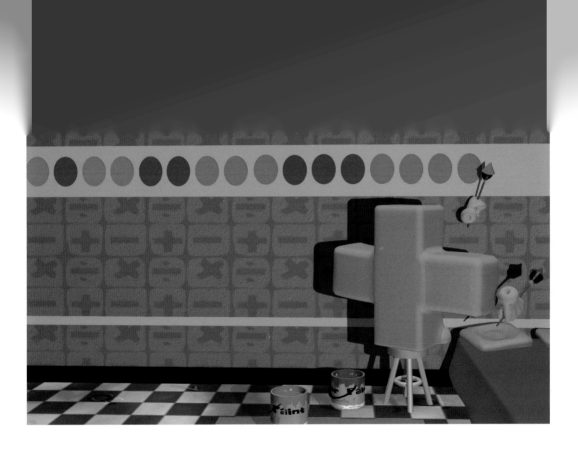

Then Addison painted four red circles.

What will Addison paint next? Why do you think so?

21

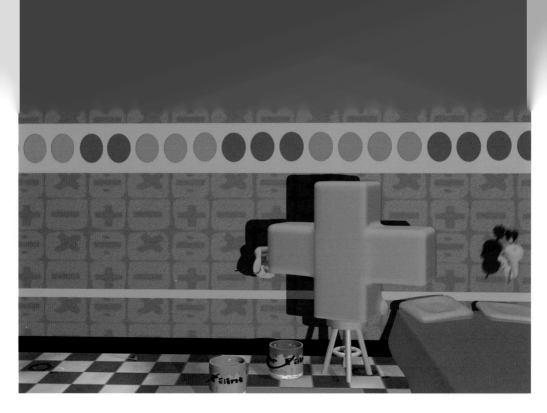

"Next," said Addison, "I will paint four blue circles."
All day long, the monsters had fun making patterns.

"I made a pattern on this cake I baked," said Mina.

"Yum!" said the monsters. "That pattern looks the best of all."

The monsters sang,
"We see patterns on cakes,
patterns on snakes,
and patterns on flakes of snow,
patterns on trees,
flowers and bees,
patterns wherever we go."

What patterns can you find in your home, at school, and outside?

23

ACTIVITIES

Page 5 Look around your home or school. Help children see patterns, such as those on wallpaper, fabric, or floors.

Pages 7, 11 Provide children with coloring tools and ask them to draw what they think Multiplex and Mina will paint.

Pages 9, 13 Discuss similarities and differences in the patterns the monsters paint. Explain that the shape many people call a diamond is actually called a rhombus.

Page 15 Cut sponges and potatoes into simple shapes. Let children enjoy using these shapes with paints to print patterns on paper. Ask them to explain where their patterns begin and end.

Pages 17, 19, 21 Making predictions and giving sound reasons for them are important mathematical skills. Ask children what they notice in a pattern that helps them decide what comes next.

Page 23 Take children on a walk through the neighborhood. Point out a variety of patterns in objects you see, such as petals on flowers or windows in buildings.